MW01100966

Morning ✳ Star

95668 Highway 101 S.
Yachats, OR 97498

CAMERON'S BOOKS
And Magazines

336 S.W. 3rd Ave.
Portland, OR 97204
503/228-2391

We Buy Books

Rachel & The Royal Garden

by

LYNDA DUMAS & JOHN DUMAS

•

ILLUSTRATED BY
LINDA GRIST D'VILLE

Cape Perpetua Press

First Edition: 1997

Printed in The United States of America

Library of Congress Catalogue Card Number: 96-86146
ISBN: 1-888934-82-4

Text copyright © 1997 by Lynda Dumas & John Dumas. All rights reserved. None of the text of this book may be used or reproduced in any manner without specific written permission, except in the case of excerpts embodied in critical articles and reviews.

Illustrations and cover design copyright © 1997 by Linda Grist D'Ville. All rights reserved. Illustrations in this book and the cover design may not be used or reproduced in any manner without specific written permission, except in the case of reproductions embodied in critical articles and reviews.

Cape Perpetua Press
A division of the Central Oregon Coast Writers' Co-op
PO Box 1012
Yachats, Oregon 97498
Tel: (541) 547-4256
E-mail: dumas@presys.com

CONTENTS

CHAPTER ONE

The Mysterious Curse

THE ROYAL GARDEN was dying, if not already dead. The leaves on the noble trees — once green and lush — were now brown and withered. They crackled in the wind like dry bones. Gone were the fruits, vegetables, and beautifully colored flowers that had abundantly supplied the King and Queen's castle for many years. The once fragrant air was filled with the stench of rotting plants. Buzzing flies swarmed everywhere. No one knew why death and decay had suddenly taken over the land. King Morland and Queen Allandra had consulted all the experts, but not one person could explain the reason the Royal Garden did not grow anymore. It seemed to be under a mysterious curse!

The rumor of a curse on the Royal Garden spread to all the villages in the Realm of Eucopia. The people of the Realm, like most people, loved to gossip, and that was how Rachel learned of the mystery. Rachel was a shy, ten-year-old girl whose Father, Mother and older brother Tod had disappeared mysteriously three years ago. Now she lived with her grandmother in a thatched-roof cottage in one of the villages.

Each day at sunrise, Rachel went to the village well to fetch water — for that was her task. One morning on her way back from the well, she stopped to listen to an agitated group of people in the village square. She was pleased no one noticed her as she stood quietly at the edge of the group with her doll, Maggie, in one hand and the wooden water bucket in the other.

"This is a burden!" said the village blacksmith in a loud angry voice. "If the Royal Garden is not rescued from this curse, we will have

Rachel listens to villagers gossiping.

to give a larger portion of our crops to the King and Queen. We can barely support our families now."

"The King and Queen have always protected us with the Royal Army in the past," said the blacksmith's wife. "We will share our food with those who are in need as long as it takes to solve the mystery of the Royal Garden."

"It's not only the Royal Garden," the blacksmith warned, "the curse is spreading like a spider's web over the entire Realm!"

"Well," his wife scolded as she patted his large round belly, "you can well afford to miss a meal or two."

The blacksmith tried to swat his wife on the rear, but she jumped out of the way. He lost his balance and stumbled clumsily. The rest of the group laughed.

"Laugh if you will," the blacksmith said as he stalked away muttering to himself. "We will see how generous you feel when your stomachs are empty."

Rachel backed away from the group hugging Maggie to her heart. She held her doll this way when she was deep in thought. *I must do something to save the Royal Garden*, she thought. *But what can I do? I'm only ten years old. If I were wise like the King and Queen, I could find an answer.* She considered that idea for a moment, then looked at Maggie with excitement. "That's it!" she shouted. "I'll go to the castle to ask the King and Queen what I can do!" That decided, she ran back to the cottage.

Rachel was nearly out of breath when she got to the cottage. She pushed open the heavy wooden door and called for her grandmother. "Grandy!" There was no answer. She set the water bucket next to the hearth and laid Maggie gently on her bed in the corner of the room. Then she looked around. A nice vegetable stew bubbled slowly in a kettle over a cozy fire in the hearth, and Grindle the cat stretched out on the window ledge sampling the early morning sun. The aroma of Grandy's scrumptious ginger cake emanated from the brick oven.

"Did Grandy go to market?" Rachel asked the sleepy-eyed cat. Grindle answered with a yawn. "Well there's no time to lose," she said.

She bent down to write a note for her grandmother in the dirt floor. Like most of the villagers, neither Rachel nor Grandy could read or write, so they used pictures for words and ideas. Rachel drew an arrow

which meant "going"; crowns which meant "King and Queen"; three suns which meant "I'll be gone three days"; and finally a heart with a smile in it which meant "I love you."

She stood back and admired her art work. She hoped that some day she could learn to read and write. "I wish the village had a school," she told Grindle. The cat answered her with another lazy yawn.

When Rachel was done, she changed into her pretty white and blue frock, a white bonnet, and put on a blue velvet cape — a special treasure from her Father. She packed some dried meats, a piece of bread, an old tin cup, and some of Grandy's ginger cake in a large blue kerchief. The ginger cake reminded Rachel of her funny brother Tod. He had loved ginger cake. But Rachel did not have time for memories. "You must not dilly-dally," she told herself. "Now what else do I need for my trip?"

Looking around, she spied a bar of soap. She wrapped it in a hand towel and placed it in the kerchief. All this fuss disturbed Grindle's catnap. He stepped gingerly from the window ledge to Grandy's old rocking chair next to the fireplace and watched Rachel with suspicious yellow eyes.

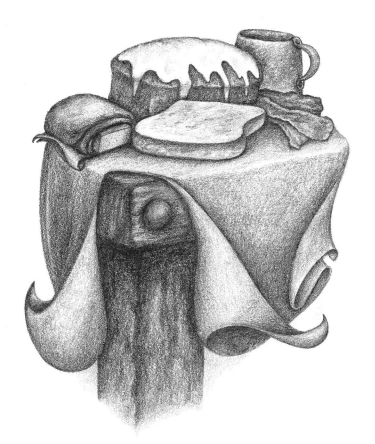

"Good-by, dear Grindle," Rachel said as she tied her kerchief in a knot. "Take care of Grandy for me while I'm gone away." She scratched the cat's ears and was rewarded with loud purrs and a raspy-tongued "cat kiss" on her hand.

The thought of leaving home brought tears to Rachel's gentle dark eyes. She went over to the bed and sat down next to her doll. "I'm so sorry, Maggie, but the journey might be too dangerous for you," she explained. "You could get hurt or lost." In some ways Rachel was too old for dolls, but Maggie had been made with loving care by her Mother and, for that reason, Rachel would never give her up.

The memories of her Mother, Father, and brother Tod brought more tears. The three family members had left on a journey to the castle one day, but they never returned. Grandy would not talk about their strange disappearance, so Rachel shared her sorrow with Maggie. Sometimes Grindle perked his ears when Rachel talked to Maggie about her loneliness. But the cat seemed to show an interest in family matters only when there were extra food scraps on the table.

Rachel sat on the bed a moment longer wiping the tears from her eyes, then quickly stood up. "But now I must go," she informed Grindle, who was already back asleep on the rocking chair. "I have things to do."

She pushed her hair in her bonnet and tied the ribbons firmly under her chin. She grabbed the blue kerchief, tossed it over her shoulder, and was off on her journey.

CHAPTER TWO

Three Wondrous Animals

RACHEL WALKED ALONG the winding dirt road leading to the castle until the sun was high overhead. She was so busy thinking about the curse on the Royal Garden she didn't realize it was lunch time until her stomach started to grumble.

She looked for a shady place to have a picnic and finally saw a crystal clear pond under a grove of trees. She skipped over to the pond and gazed in it. The water was smooth like a looking glass and she could see her own reflection. *This looks quite clean*, she thought. She sat down under a tree, opened her kerchief, and dipped the tin cup into the pond. She took a sip of water and began eating some of the bread and dried meats she had brought along. A soft breeze whispered through the leaves and cooled her rosy cheeks. It was all very peaceful.

Rachel was almost finished with lunch and had picked up a piece of ginger cake when, suddenly, a wet brown toad jumped out of the pond and landed next to her with a splash. *SHLOP!* She was so startled she dropped the ginger cake. "My goodness!" she exclaimed, and reached for the ginger cake.

"Sorry, Sport — Sport, sorry," croaked the toad.

"You can talk!" screamed Rachel, dropping the ginger cake again. She quickly grabbed the cake and jumped up. She began slowly backing away from the wet toad, but bumped her head against a low branch on the tree.

"Oops-a-daisy — daisy-oops!" sputtered the toad. "Don't be scared of happy-go-lucky me — me lucky-go-happy scared be don't,"

he continued. He earnestly bobbed his thick brown head up and down, spraying water everywhere.

Rachel rubbed the back of her head. "I've never heard of a talking toad before," she said. "You must be very special."

"Very special, Sport — Sport, special very." He smiled a large toad grin. "I am captain of this pond — pond captain am I."

"Captains guide ships," Rachel corrected, "not ponds."

"Guiding this pond's a hardship — hardship a pond's guiding," he replied, "That's ship enough for me — me for enough ship. And you know, Sport…"

"My name is Rachel, Captain Toad," she interrupted, "not Sport." Her glaring eyes and wrinkled forehead indicated her growing anger for this strange animal's lack of manners. Grandy would certainly not approve of bad manners even from a toad — at least not from a *talking* toad.

"Sorry, Spor…I mean, sorry, *Rachel — Rachel*, sorry mean I," Captain Toad answered happily — paying no attention to Rachel's frown. "Anyway, I know for a fact that all animals can talk — talk can animals all." Captain Toad grinned again.

"They can?" asked Rachel skeptically, forgetting her anger.

"Only when there's something to say — say to something," the toad replied. "That's the difference — difference that."

"Difference?" Rachel questioned.

"Between animals and humans — humans and animals," Captain Toad explained. "Humans talk when there's *nothing* to say — say to nothing."

"Humans talk when there's nothing to say?" repeated Rachel.

"Done all the time — time all done," said the toad.

"Then what do humans do when there's *something* to say?" Rachel asked.

"They're utterless — utterless they," Captain Toad answered, "Until there's nothing to say — say to nothing."

Rachel was confused. "Humans don't speak when there's *something* to say, but when there's *nothing* to say…"

"…they pipe right up — up right pipe," the toad finished for her. He blinked his huge watery eyes. *SQUISH! SQUISH!*

This toad sees things topsy-turvy, Rachel thought. *And says things topsy-turvy too.* "Why do you repeat backwards what you say forwards?" she asked.

"Because of yonder pond — pond yonder," said the toad.

"The pond?" said Rachel.

"It's a reflecting pond — pond reflecting," said Captain Toad. "I do a lot of reflecting — reflecting lot do I."

"Reflecting?" asked Rachel.

"Same as pondering — pondering as same," he explained.

"You ponder?" she questioned.

"Ponder on yonder pond —," he croaked, "pond yonder on ponder."

She eyed the toad warily. "But sometimes your backwards words are not exactly a reflection of your forwards words," she carefully observed.

"Tis true — true tis," he admitted. "Sometimes I speak without reflecting — reflecting without speak. Tis almost human — human almost."

Rachel was not sure what to think of Captain Toad. *He speaks nonsense*, she thought, *but after all, he's only a toad. Just because he talks, doesn't make him smart.* "If animals seldom talk," she challenged, "why are you talking to me?"

"Around here we see few ginger cakes — cakes ginger few see we," Captain Toad said. "I dearly love ginger cake — cake ginger love I."

"Ginger cake?" asked Rachel. "I believe toads are supposed to like flies."

"Flies are okay I suppose — suppose I okay flies," he said. "But if I could choose — choose could I," he continued, glancing eagerly at the ginger cake, "I'd take the cake — cake take I."

Well, thought Rachel, *this toad certainly does take the cake.* "I don't have much," she said, "but you're certainly welcome to share with me." She broke the ginger cake in two and held the bigger piece out to Captain Toad.

"Thank you — you thank!" sputtered

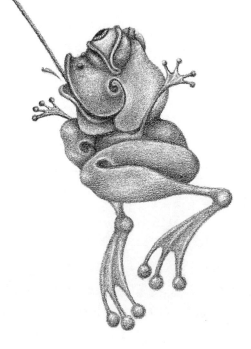

the toad. "If ever you need a favor, just call on me — me on call." He blinked his eyes again. *SQUISH! SQUISH!* Then his lightning-fast tongue whipped the ginger cake out of Rachel's hand and into his mouth before she could blink. His cheeks puffed out with delight.

Rachel did not think a toad could ever help her, but she sat down next to him and had a lovely time finishing her meal while he munched merrily on the ginger cake. No one talked.

After lunch, Rachel laid her head on the kerchief for a short nap. Captain

Rachel and Captain Toad enjoy ginger cake.

Toad sat on a toadstool nearby to warn her in case of danger. But there was no danger, and when she awoke, Captain Toad was gone. She rubbed her eyes, picked up her kerchief, and resumed her journey to the castle.

As she walked, Rachel began to wonder if her encounter with Captain Toad had all been a dream. *No one in the village would believe me,* she thought. *I'll tell only Grindle and Maggie, and make them keep it a secret.* She was so deep in thought that she wandered off the road and almost stepped on a baby bird that had fallen from its nest. At the last second, the mother bird flew in front of Rachel's foot to keep her from stepping on the fledgling.

"Look out!" squealed Mother Bird, flapping her gray wings in alarm. "For not only has my baby — *CHIRP!* — fallen out of his home, it looks like now he'll be squashed! I don't know how — *CHIRP!* — I'll get him back up into the nest." Mother Bird was a gray blur as she flew frantically back and forth from her baby to the nest, chirping with alarm.

Oh, oh, thought Rachel, *another talking animal.* "Don't worry, Mother Bird." she said. "I'll be glad to help you." The baby bird had fallen from its nest and its tiny wing was caught between two large stones. Rachel gently moved the stones and lifted the baby bird back to the nest.

Mother Bird flew to the nest to check on her little one. Then she swooped down and landed on Rachel's still outstretched hand. "My baby will be okay," chirped Mother Bird. "Thank you so much for your kindness."

"I really did very little," said Rachel.

"It wasn't very little to me," replied Mother Bird. "You saved my little one. Besides, doing a kind deed — *CHIRP!* — isn't as easy as you might think. For many humans, it's absolutely impossible."

"But," protested Rachel, "the villagers often speak of people doing kind deeds."

Mother Bird tilted her head and looked at Rachel. "How old — *CHIRP!* — are you, my dear?"

"I'm ten years old," said Rachel. "And my name is Rachel."

Rachel talks with Mother Bird.

"Well, Rachel," said Mother Bird tenderly, "humans see only what they're meant to see, but birds see much more."

"What do you mean?" Rachel asked.

"It's easy for humans to do kind deeds that other humans will see and praise," Mother Bird explained. "But kind deeds that can only be viewed from a bird's eye, — *CHIRP!* — humans find much more difficult. In fact, many humans find such kind deeds quite impossible. So I thank you."

A kind deed impossible? thought Rachel. Mother Bird didn't seem to make much sense, but the gentle creature had only the brain of a bird, so Rachel didn't contradict her. "Well, you are entirely welcome, Mother Bird," she said with a warm smile.

Mother Bird crossed her wings in front of her feathered body. "Rachel, my dear, if ever you need help — *CHIRP!* — please call for me." With that, she flew up to her nest.

Rachel thought that the good-hearted bird couldn't do much to help her, but then she had an idea. "How far from here is the King and Queen's castle?" she asked.

Mother Bird got a worried look on her brow. "You won't arrive at the castle — *CHIRP!* — before nightfall," she said.

"Please don't worry," Rachel said. "I'll be okay." She waved a friendly good-bye and set foot on the road to the castle once more.

Rachel walked all afternoon, but as evening approached, she decided to find a place to sleep so she could arrive well-rested at the castle in the morning. Soon she found a nice pile of fallen leaves by a babbling brook. As the sky darkened, she gathered more leaves and added them to the pile to make a soft bed. She spread her kerchief, which was quite large, over the leaves as a bottom cover and placed her cape over the kerchief as a top cover. Finally, she stuffed a few leaves in her bonnet for a pillow. Satisfied with her lovely new bed, Rachel took the bar of soap and went over to the brook to wash up for supper.

She carefully washed her hands and had just started to rinse them when a booming voice echoed through the forest. "Can you provide some justification for your uninvited presence here?"

Rachel gasped and jumped to her feet. She searched in the direction of the voice, but could see nothing in the dimming light. Then she noticed her wet hands dripping water on her favorite frock. "Oh, no!" she cried out.

"*No* justification?" the voice rumbled.

"No! No! I don't mean *that*." pleaded Rachel. "It is just if the water were not on my frock..."

"Just-if-the-water is not justification," the voice answered. It had moved.

Rachel had to turn to face the thundering sound. "Where are you?" she asked.

"I happen to be in a new position at the moment!" bellowed the voice.

Rachel looked into the dark shadows of the forest, but could see nothing. "Why is someone with such a large voice so afraid to be seen?" Rachel finally demanded. She had forgotten the water drops on her frock.

"The larger the elk, the more he should fear the hunter," answered the voice.

"Oh, Mister Elk," Rachel said. "I'm not a hunter." She was not surprised to be talking to another animal. "I'm just a ten year old girl named Rachel. Please stop moving about. I promise not to harm you."

Cautiously from the shadows where Rachel had been looking emerged a large, powerful elk. His sleek golden fur glowed in the fading light of day. On his head was a tremendous rack of antlers. "Young girls believe in promises," he said. "Yours is a promise I can trust."

Rachel looked at the elk indignantly. "Everyone believes in promises," she protested. "A promise *is* a promise."

"I beg to differ," said Mister Elk. "All promises are not the same. A young girl's promise is stronger than bronze, but a king's promise is more fragile than glass."

Rachel was appalled at the irreverent elk. "Promises of mighty kings are the most powerful of all!" she quickly corrected him in a firm voice.

"If so," said Mister Elk, "why are promises of kings the most easily broken?"

Mister Elk is so busy hiding from hunters, Rachel thought, *that he has no time to understand promises and kings.* But Grandy once told her only fools argue with ignorance, so Rachel didn't disagree with the elk. "You must do a lot of thinking," she finally said, "to have such strong opinions."

"Ruminating," he answered. "It is an occupational hazard for ruminants."

"Ruminating?" Rachel inquired.

"That is the difference between ruminants and humans," he said.

"Difference?" she echoed.

"Humans swallow opinions without much analysis," he explained. "But ruminants chew over opinions quite carefully before accepting them."

This all sounded like nonsense to Rachel, but she thought it disrespectful to say so. Instead, she told Mister Elk about the mysterious curse on the Royal Garden and how it was important for her to do something about it. "I don't know what I can do," she explained, "but I must at least try."

Mister Elk listened carefully to her story, all the while trying to rub his head on a tree trunk even though his large antlers kept getting in the way.

Rachel meets Mister Elk.

"Why are you doing that?" Rachel inquired.

"Because a diminutive leaf blew in my ear and I cannot get it out," he grumbled. "It is really quite bothersome."

"Let me see," requested Rachel. The powerful animal bent his huge head down toward the girl and cocked his ear for her to see. Rachel got up on her tip toes and inspected the elk's ear. "Here it is," she said. "Please hold still…I think I can reach it…There!" she exclaimed victoriously, and held the annoying leaf in front of Mister Elk's large brown eyes.

"Thank you so much!" said the elk. "I cannot tell you how terribly annoying something can be when it is quite in reach, but impossible to do anything about."

"You're welcome," said Rachel.

"Dear girl," Mister Elk continued, "please know that if there is ever a time in the future when you may have need for any type of assistance, just call out and perhaps I may be able to do a similar service for you in return."

Well, considered Rachel, *Mister Elk certainly spills a lot of words when he pours out a thought, but I think I like him best.* She could not imagine how an elk who could not even get a leaf out of his ear could ever be of help, but she did not say so. "You have my promise" she agreed. "Now I

18

must fix my supper and then rest up for the journey tomorrow."

"Certainly, Rachel," said Mister Elk. "Sweet dreams." And with a powerful bound he disappeared into the forest.

This is going to be hard to explain to Grandy, Rachel thought while climbing onto her bed of leaves. *Three animals talked to me today! And each of them promised to help me if ever I am in need. Maybe this is an omen that somehow I'll be able to help the King and Queen.* And with these good thoughts, Rachel fell asleep. She did not know that Mister Elk stood nearby in the forest guarding her resting place.

CHAPTER THREE

Three Impossible Tasks

RACHEL AWOKE EARLY the next morning to the beginning of a beautiful day. She dressed quickly and set out on her journey once again. She enjoyed walking through the Royal Forest, but the closer she got to the castle, the more barren and parched everything became. The curse on the Royal Garden was spreading over the entire Realm!

She did not meet any more talking animals along the way, but she saw the Royal cattle and sheep when she got to the Royal Pasture. It was dry and dusty, and the animals had no food. They were bony and gazed at her with large hungry eyes.

The animals are so thin they look like skeletons, she thought. *And their faces are so sad.* She was more determined than ever to help save the Realm from the mysterious curse.

While Rachel was looking at the gloomy condition of the Royal Pasture, a shiny black coach pulled by six black horses roared by without warning. *CARROOM!-BADOOM!-BADOOM!*

The wind from the passing coach blew her over like a rag doll and left her sitting in a cloud of dust.

"That coach is certainly in a hurry," she said to the unresponsive pasture animals.

Choking back the dust, she got to her feet and brushed herself off. As she looked to see where the coach had gone she saw a fantastic sight. "There it is!" she shouted. Just over a low hill rising high over all the countryside she saw the top of the immense castle tower. Her heart

Rachel sees the castle tower.

skipped a beat. Her journey was almost over! In her excitement she forgot about the black coach and started hurrying toward the castle.

As Rachel approached the high castle walls, she wondered how she would get inside. She had never visited a castle before. She saw a monstrous wooden gate and walked toward it. Just outside the gate she saw the black coach that had knocked her down. The six black horses were panting and sweating. Two Royal Guards had opened the gate slightly and were busy talking to someone inside the coach. They did not notice the young girl in the blue cape. Rachel quietly tip-toed past the coach and the Royal Guards and kept going through the gate right into the castle courtyard. It was really very easy. *That problem is solved*, she thought.

Once inside the castle courtyard, Rachel looked up in awe at the gigantic rock walls and the soaring tower that seemed to touch the sky. Everything was so large and tall it made her dizzy. *How could a small girl like me save this mighty Realm?* she thought. She felt weak and helpless. She did not see how she could save the Royal Garden. It would not be right for a young girl to bother the King and Queen with such a silly idea. She was so lost in her thoughts she did not notice a large gathering of people at the far end of the courtyard. Suddenly, the crowd erupted in a loud cheer. "HURRAH!" Rachel blinked with surprise and took a quick breath. *What is all the fuss about?* she wondered. She cautiously walked over to the commotion to see what was happening.

The crowd was gathered at the bottom of the stairs leading up to the entrance to the King and Queen's majestic Royal Chambers. At the top of the stairs stood King Morland and Queen Allandra who had just stepped out into the sunlight. Their purple robes were dazzling. Rachel's stomach churned with excitement. The crowd continued to cheer until King Morland finally raised his hands and everyone fell silent.

"Good people," said the King, "we still have not solved the curse on the Royal Garden." The crowd let out a moan.

"Your Majesty," shouted a very important-sounding man, "I have been studying the Royal Garden and grounds and I do not think the reason is one of nature. It is definitely the work of a witch or sorcerer or the like." The man then crossed his arms over his chest and half-closed his eyes in self-satisfaction, as if expecting the crowd to applaud him. *He seems quite certain of his opinion*, Rachel thought. *He must specialize in curses on royal gardens.*

"Thank you, Good Fellow Sharlatan," replied the King. "I believe you are correct. The Royal Advisors have told me that this is the only possible explanation." Queen Allandra nodded her head in agreement. As she did so, her soft hair shimmered merrily in the sun, but her face was sad. King Morland took hold of her hand.

Just then the shiny black coach roared into the middle of the courtyard raising a billowing cloud of dust. The wheels made a horrible clatter and the horses whinnied and snorted. A look of concern came over King Morland's face. He led Queen Allandra down the stairs to the coach. The crowd watched in fearful silence. The coach was driven by two footmen who wore black hats and gold velvet coats studded with dark purple jewels. *If this is what the footmen wear*, thought Rachel, *I can hardly wait to see the passenger!* She got on her toes and stretched her neck to see who was getting out of the coach.

The crowd held its breath as all eyes were focused on the door of the coach. Time seemed to stand still. Finally, the gleaming black door opened. The onlookers gasped. The interior of the coach was lined with dark red velvet — the color of blood. Then a cold white hand, covered with jewels, reached out and grasped the gloved hand of a footman, and out stepped a woman dressed in a brilliant white gown with rich purple trim. Her flaming red hair was sprinkled with flashing diamonds

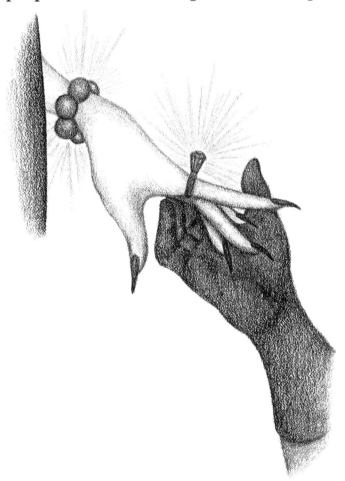

as if her head were on fire. She looked dazzling and beautiful — almost as beautiful as Queen Allandra. The strange woman stood above the crowd on the coach step and glared menacingly down at the King. Rachel was spellbound by the woman's mysterious emerald-green eyes.

"So *she* is the Sorceress," King Morland whispered to himself. "Now I understand what has been happening to the Realm."

The mouth of the Sorceress twisted into a wicked smile. "I told you three years ago that I would get even with you for choosing Allandra over me," she said. "And I am more powerful now than I was then."

The crowd murmured nervously and drew back from the coach. The six horses snorted and pawed the dust restlessly. The Sorceress waved her hand and immediately silenced the mighty beasts. Rachel's eyes widened at the woman's wondrous power.

"I shall introduce myself to the people of the Realm," the Sorceress declared to King Morland. She gazed on the crowd with contempt. "Lowly peasants, my name is Arachne…" she began.

"You are under arrest!" yelled a Royal Guard who came running into the courtyard from the castle gate. "You have entered the castle without permission." He started to reach for Arachne, but King Morland held up his hand to stop him.

"It is no use," the King told the Royal Guard. "If you touch her ever so slightly your hand will burst into flames and burn forever." The crowd shuddered in horror and shrank back further from the coach.

Arachne flashed her emerald-green eyes at the Royal Guard, then continued. "When I was a young girl, my father made a contract with the father of your King that I would marry his only son, Morland, and become Queen. But three years ago, your kind and gentle King," — with these words she looked mockingly at King Morland — "your true and trustworthy Morland fell in love with the fair Allandra," — she pointed her long spidery finger at Queen Allandra — "for the foolish reason that she has a kind heart. Now *she* is Queen instead of me! To get out of the contract to marry me, your King gave my father a plot of land."

Arachne's fierce emerald-green eyes began to glow like eerie flames. "DIRT!" she screamed. "YOUR KING THINKS I AM WORTH NOTHING MORE THAN DIRT!"

The onlookers recoiled and turned their eyes cautiously to King Morland.

"But dirt can be quite valuable," Arachne continued after a theatrical pause. "For without it, you can grow nothing. To show just how 'dear' dirt can be, I have spun a curse — a gossamer curse that shall spread like a spider's web over all the King and Queen's land. Soon, nothing shall grow in the entire Realm!"

Good King Morland stepped forward. "Punish me if you must," he pleaded with Arachne, "but it is not fair to punish these innocent people."

"Do you fail to see?" Arachne answered scornfully. "Punishing the people of the Realm is punishing you. You care too much for them. I predict that not one of them would volunteer to save the Realm from this curse."

"The people of the Realm are all loyal," said the King, "and would do whatever they could to save it."

"To prove you wrong," Arachne sneered, "I offer you this challenge. The curse shall be broken if one person performs Three Impossible Tasks — difficult tasks which are quite beyond the feeble powers of a simple human." She held up three spidery fingers and smiled a wicked smile. "The Three Impossible Tasks must be performed without the help of any other human. If that person fails at any one of the Three Impossible Tasks — or if my instructions are not followed to the letter — the poor wretch shall shrivel up like a leaf in autumn and die like the Royal Garden."

The onlookers stirred uneasily. Queen Allandra clasped King Morland's hand. "Sire, perhaps I should leave the Realm," she offered. "Perhaps then Arachne will release the curse and the people of the Realm will not have to suffer."

"It is too late for sentimental sacrifices, my dear Allandra," snarled Arachne. "The spell has been cast over the land, and there is only one

way to save it. If one of your loyal people accomplishes the Three Impossible Tasks, the Realm shall be restored and my powers forever destroyed. But I am not worried." She looked at the trembling crowd, her emerald-green eyes gleaming vengefully. "Which of you loyal people dares to take this challenge?"

No one spoke. The crowd was deathly silent.

Rachel could not believe her ears. She looked around at the grown-ups. None of them offered to take on Arachne's Three Impossible Tasks — not even the pompous Good Fellow Sharlatan. The Realm was doomed! Suddenly without thinking, Rachel ran through the wobbling legs of the onlookers and up to Arachne's coach.

"Exc...uhm...excuse me, please..." Rachel whispered haltingly.

Arachne peered down at the shy girl in the blue cape. "Who is this little trembling waif?" she screeched. "Do not tell me, King Morland, that a feeble child is the only person with any spirit!" She burst into a malicious cackle. "Very well, I will give her the First Impossible Task. It is nothing to me."

"Dear Girl," said King Morland to Rachel, "you heard Arachne. You must not place yourself in danger. I shall try to think of a way out of this. Please go back to your home where it is safe. I am certain your parents are worried about you."

"Your Majesty," said Rachel with a shaky voice, "I fear I no longer have parents — my Mother, my Father, and my brother Tod have been missing for three years. I've come from my grandmother's cottage to help you. I would like to try. People say I'm quite clever and perhaps I'll be able to do the Three Impossible Tasks. I'm not afraid." *At least not very afraid*, she thought.

"Let her try," shouted Arachne. "I find it most amusing that your pathetic hero should be an orphaned child. It is a pity her life shall be so short." She laughed again and her jeweled red hair danced in the blazing sun.

29

"Dear child," spoke the King, "you will die if you fail! Please go back to your village. Arachne is far too eager that you try the Three Impossible Tasks. There is no way for you to beat her. I do thank you for wanting to help." King Morland patted Rachel kindly on the shoulder.

"Your Majesty," said Rachel, "I made up my mind to help and I shall do so. If I fail, then at least I've tried. Grandy says that a person should never live in fear of trying."

"Oh, very well," sighed the King. "I will not be able to talk you out of this, I see. The Three Impossible Tasks are yours."

Arachne clapped her hands. "Wonderful!" she said. "We shall begin. What is the name of our foolhardy little heroine?"

30

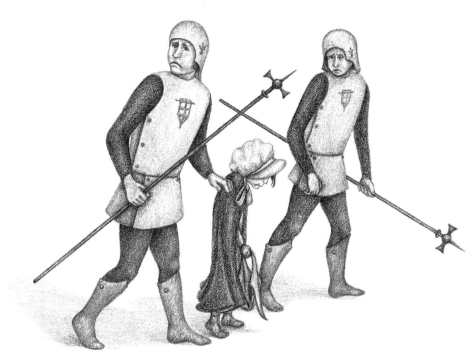

"My name is Rachel," Rachel replied bravely.

"All right, Rachel," Arachne said with a false smile. "The First Impossible Task shall be this: There is an enchanted tree which grows in the Forest of Coriola in a far-off corner of the Realm. One of the tree's boughs is made of solid bronze. The bronze bough sprouts leaves of pure silver and bears a single apple of solid gold. It is the richest treasure in the Realm. You must bring this bough to me by sunrise tomorrow. No one has ever been able to remove the bronze bough from the enchanted tree, not even my father's mightiest knights. Further, you are to do this while locked in a room at the castle under guard! And remember, no other human may help you."

The crowd flinched in horror. Such an outrageous task meant certain death. Rachel felt sick. *I don't think I can help the King and Queen after all*, she thought. *This task truly is impossible!*

Obediently, the Royal Guards came forward and marched Rachel to a room at the back of the castle.

Arachne watched Rachel disappear into the castle, then stepped into her coach. "I shall see you all at sunrise!" she said with a laugh. As her coach rushed out the castle gate, she shouted to the King and Queen — "Tomorrow, your little girl blue shall wither and die!"

The King and Queen looked sadly at one another. It did not seem right that their Realm and a young girl should suffer because of their happiness.

"Come," said King Morland to Queen Allandra. "Let us talk

with the Royal Magicians. Perhaps they can find a way to accomplish the First Impossible Task."

CHAPTER FOUR

The Bronze Bough

RACHEL HEARD THE rasping of a metal key outside the door as the Royal Guard locked her in a room on the ground floor of the castle. The room had one barred window. Through the bars she could see the withered trees and plants of the Royal Garden. She had heard tales of travelers who came from far and wide to see the magnificent beauty of the Royal Garden. But now there were no visitors. The Royal Garden was parched and ugly. Rotten fruit and vegetables littered the ground. The air had a foul odor and was filled with buzzing flies — flies so thick that it was difficult to see the Royal Forest beyond.

Rachel turned away from the window and inspected her room. The Royal Guards had left a lunch on a table for her — but she was not hungry. Across the room from the window was a lumpy bed. She went over to the bed and sat down. It was time to think.

What shall I do? It is quite impossible to win the bronze bough with silver leaves and a golden apple without leaving this room. To do that I would have to be a sorceress myself!

Rachel thought and thought, but she could not hit upon a plan. And the longer she thought, the sadder she became. She began crying softly and scolded herself that tears would accomplish nothing. But her sobs sailed out through the bars on the window into the Royal Garden. From there, the wind carried them deep into the Royal Forest where Mister Elk was ruminating. His alert ears picked up the troubled sounds.

"What on earth is creating that disturbance?" he said when he heard the crying. "I believe an investigation is in order." He bounded through the forest and over the dried up wasteland of the Royal Garden toward the sound of the sobbing. When he came to the barred window at the back of the castle he was surprised to find his new friend locked in a room.

"Good afternoon, Rachel" he called. "May I be of any assistance?"

Rachel jumped up from her bed and ran to the window. She was very happy to see her ruminating friend. "Oh, Mister Elk," she cried. "I'm so glad to see you." She brushed the tears from her eyes.

"What is the foundation for these whimperings and waterworks?" he said with a concerned look in his large brown eyes. Rachel told him about Arachne and the bronze bough that sprang from an enchanted tree and sprouted silver leaves and a golden apple.

Mister Elk listened calmly and when she finished he spoke up. "Stop your crying, my dear girl! Dry your eyes this minute. This provides me with an opportunity to reciprocate your kindness to me." He turned his head for a moment to remind her of the pesky leaf she had removed from his ear.

"The forest is my home and I can find the enchanted tree," he continued. "Precious metals are frivolous human treasures. They are worth nothing to sensible forest creatures. I would gladly bring you the bronze bough with silver leaves and a golden apple."

"But," cried Rachel, "the mightiest knights could not remove it from the enchanted tree."

"Do not let the tales of errant knights beguile you," responded Mister Elk. "Their valor is often exceeded by their imagination. I promise to bring you the precious bough." And before Rachel could say another word, he was off.

Rachel sat down again on the bed. *Mr. Elk promised to bring me the bough*, she thought, *and he takes promises quite seriously.* Her mind was so jumbled with the events of the day she couldn't concentrate. She could think only of Mister Elk's kind brown eyes. She laid her head on the pillow and was soon fast asleep, dreaming about her long-lost Father.

~

AFTER LEAVING RACHEL, Mister Elk bounded swiftly through the forests of the Realm, and reached the Forest of Coriola — where the enchanted tree was located — by early evening. He was thirsty and breathing hard from the run. He stopped and drank deeply the cool water from a clear stream.

Soon his breathing slowed to normal and he began looking for the enchanted tree. He walked in ever widening circles until he spotted a glowing golden gleam through the thick forest. He trotted through the brush toward the gleam and came upon the enchanted tree. The brilliant bronze bough with silver leaves and a golden apple was so dazzling he could hardly look at it. He could see cuts and slashes in the sturdy trunk of the tree made by the axes of the knights, but there was not a scratch on the bronze bough itself. *Axes are not the answer*, he thought.

Mister Elk immediately began calculating how to dislodge the bronze bough from the enchanted tree. He walked around the large old tree and studied the way the bronze bough grew from the thick brown trunk. The cuts and slashes made by the knights' axes in the trunk were all above the bronze bough. There were no marks on the trunk below it.

The knights have been unable to cut the bronze bough from the top, he observed, *perhaps the underside is weaker and I would have better luck from below.* It did seem to look weaker to him — but not much.

Mister Elk stood beneath the bronze bough and placed his mighty antlers under it. He pushed up to test its strength. It did not budge. He could see that it was not going to be easy. He placed his front hooves on a gnarled root for better leverage. He took a deep breath and strained with all his might upward against the bronze bough. He heard something give in the tree. *CRICK!* But the bronze bough remained firm. Exhausted, he stepped away from the enchanted tree to catch his breath. His golden coat glistened with sweat.

After catching his breath, Mister Elk again placed himself under the bronze bough. He took in an even bigger breath and, with a thundering bellow, thrust up against it with all his might. "HAAARRRUUUMMMFFF!" The forest rocked and the enchanted tree groaned once more. *CARRICK-ICK-ICK!* But the bronze bough did not budge.

Mister Elk became disheartened. He dropped his head in gloom. Maybe he would *not* be able to keep the promise he made to Rachel. This task *did* seem impossible. Mighty knights had not been able to dislodge the bronze bough — no one could blame an elk for not doing so.

Sometimes there is justification for not keeping a promise, he reasoned. *But is it justification…or just-a-vacation…from keeping one's word?* He knew that many persons who failed to accomplish difficult tasks often had good excuses. For them, such tasks were impossible. What puzzled Mister Elk was that other persons with exactly the same good excuses

Mister Elk tries to dislodge the Bronze Bow.

were able to accomplish the same "impossible" tasks. *Tasks are always impossible if a person does not try,* he thought. He raised his mighty head. "Sometimes there is justification for not keeping a promise," he announced to the enchanted tree, "but there is *never* justification for not *trying* to keep a promise." His mind was made up.

Mister Elk strode purposefully back to the stream and took another deep drink of the cool water. He paused for a short time to recover his strength. Then, with determined steps he walked back to the stubborn tree. He planted his hoofs firmly on the exposed root. His strong hind legs flexed as his back hooves dug into the forest floor.

Either the bronze bough breaks or I break! he decided. He placed his mighty antlers under the bronze bough, took a tremendous breath, and thrust up against it with all his being. He strained until it seemed his bulging muscles would explode. His body ached. His head throbbed. But he pushed even harder. *If Rachel must die, so shall I,* he thought.

Suddenly the forest shuddered and echoed with a deafening sound. *KRAAABOOOOOM-OOM-OOM!* Mister Elk felt the bronze bough break away from the enchanted tree. He tumbled over backward as the prize shot high into the air and out of sight. "I have done it!" he bellowed, panting on the forest floor. "I have accomplished the task!"

But Mister Elk's problems were not over. Night had fallen and he did not see where the bronze bough had gone. *This is a fine piece of work,* he thought. *I have succeeded in knocking the precious bronze bough from the enchanted tree, only to lose it in the forest! How will I ever be able to find it in the dark in time to get it back to Rachel before sunrise! Worrying will certainly not find it — I shall start looking.*

He examined where the bronze bough had broken off from the trunk of the enchanted tree and where he had fallen. From that, he calculated in which direction it might have flown. With this clue, he started an anxious search for the bronze bough in the black forest.

~

WHILE MR. ELK searched the forest, Rachel slept. She was exhausted. Her troubling encounter with Arachne and all her other adventures were more than a young girl could endure. She slept restlessly through the night until the next morning when a loud knock on the locked door startled her from her sleep.

"Time to get up, Rachel," called a Royal Guard from the other side of the door. Rachel blinked the sleep from her eyes and looked around. *Where am I?* she wondered. Then she saw the barred window. She remembered Arachne, the bronze bough, and Mister Elk. *It's almost sunrise and he's not back*, she thought. *The Royal Garden won't be saved!* Then her eye caught sight of something shining on the floor just below the window. It was a brilliant golden apple surrounded by silver leaves and attached to a bronze bough! It glowed strangely in the early morning light. "That's it!" she screamed with excitement. "Mister Elk must have dropped it through the window while I was asleep."

Rachel hopped out of bed and ran over to the treasure. She could not believe her eyes. She peered out the window to thank Mister

39

Elk, but could not see him anywhere. She lifted the wonderful bronze bough and held it in her arms. It was quite heavy. *Mr. Elk does believe in promises*, she thought.

Suddenly she realized that it was almost sunrise. She heard the castle gates open and a coach rumble into the courtyard. She set the  bronze bough on the bed and quickly dressed, washed her face, brushed her teeth and combed her hair. Just as she finished, there was another knock on the door.

"Rachel," called the King. "I am afraid it is time." His voice sounded very sad.

"Ready, Your Majesty!" Rachel called. She could hardly hide her excitement. She picked up the bronze bough and skipped over to the door just as it was opening.

"I fear you did not spend a pleasant night…" the King started to say. But then he saw the beaming smile on Rachel's face and the glowing bronze bough in her arms. His eyes opened wide as he cried, "Rachel, you have done it! I know not how, but you have indeed secured the treasure!" He took the heavy bronze bough from her and handed it to the Royal Guard. Then he did something very un-kingly. He picked Rachel up in his arms and swung her around the room. "Let us keep our engagement with that horrible woman," he said.

Rachel and the King walked into the courtyard followed by the Royal Guard carrying the magnificent bronze bough. As the first rays of the morning sun peeked over the castle wall, they beamed off of the golden apple with blinding brilliance. It was so bright that Queen Allandra and the waiting crowd had to look away. Arachne, who stood with a vicious smile on the coach step, screeched and covered her eyes with her hands. Then she slowly took her hands away and saw the bronze bough. She grew furious. "What kind of trick is this?" she demanded. She clenched her fists in anger and hid them in the folds of her resplendent silver and gold gown.

The King and Rachel arrived at Arachne's coach. The Royal Guard followed and placed the bronze bough on the step where Arachne stood. She angrily ordered her footmen to place the brilliant treasure inside. An anxious crowd watched as the astonished footmen quickly set the bronze bough on the red velvet seat.

Arachne became very impatient. "So," she cried, "I see you have succeeded in the First Impossible Task! Tell me, Rachel," she asked suspiciously, "are you a witch?" Arachne's emerald-green eyes glared at Rachel, who was very frightened of this demanding Sorceress.

"No, I'm not a w-w-witch," she stammered. "I f-f-followed your rules and was not helped by any h-h-human." Rachel was very pale and her voice quavered.

"Liar!" Arachne shrieked. "The Royal Magicians must have helped you. No, wait — they are as useless as you." She stared angrily at the crowd and stamped her foot. "Just who *did* help this puny girl?" she screamed.

King Morland smiled calmly. "As you instructed, no human helped Rachel with the First Impossible Task. We are as puzzled as you." He turned to Rachel, who was starting to get some of the color back in her cheeks. "Dear girl, just how did you manage this?" he asked gently.

"Yes, you horrid child," screamed Arachne. "Just how did you perform this task without magic?"

"I was helped by Mister Elk..." Rachel started to explain.

"An elk!" Arachne interrupted. "A stupid beast of the forest! Just why would an elk help you!"

Rachel began to get angry with Arachne because she was so loud and rude. "I will tell you if you will just be quiet," Rachel stated firmly.

"That's telling the shrew, Rachel!" hollered a voice from the crowd. Everyone gasped.

Hmm, that voice sounds very familiar, thought Rachel. She peered into the crowd and saw a small woman with fire in her eyes staring at Arachne. It was Rachel's grandmother. "Grandy!" Rachel cried out with joy. "It's you!"

Grandy rushed forward through the astonished onlookers and put her arms around Rachel. "There, there," she soothed. "When I saw your message, I just had to come to be with you and see if there was something I could do."

"So this meddling hag helped you," Arachne said, pointing an accusing finger at Grandy.

"I did not, you old bat," Grandy answered.

The crowd gasped again in stunned disbelief. The King and Queen tried to hide their smiles.

Arachne's face turned a burning red to match her hair. "Enjoy your little moment," she said slowly and quietly to Grandy, "but I would like to hear the rest of this impudent imp's story."

"Just because you're upset is no reason to treat a person with dis-respect," Rachel challenged.

Arachne glared at Rachel. "All right, my dear," she finally said in a vicious whisper. "Please go on with your story."

Rachel held onto Grandy's hand and continued her story. "On my journey to see the King and Queen, I did a favor for Mister Elk. Then, yesterday, he heard me crying in the locked room and came to the window to see if he could help. I told him about the bronze bough with the silver leaves and golden apple. He knew the forest well and was sure he could find the enchanted tree. He promised to bring me the bronze bough. This morning when I awoke, it was on the floor of the room below the window. I believe he used his brains and powerful antlers to break it off the enchanted tree. By the way, like most forest creatures, Mister Elk is not stupid — he's very smart."

"He just used his head!" Grandy shouted at Arachne.

A few muffled snickers escaped from the crowd.

Arachne glared at Grandy with disgust. "So," she said, looking back at Rachel, "you shall live one more day, my little pest. Therefore, it is time to give you the Second Impossible Task."

Arachne paused to make sure she had everyone's attention. Then she spoke.

"There is a cottage at the very top of the highest mountain in the snow-covered Kingdom of Rezonantz. In that cottage lives a fierce Giant and his cook. Somewhere hidden in the cottage is a most wonderful jewel. No one has ever been able to reach the jewel because it is guarded by the Giant. Those who have been silly enough to try to scale the mountain and capture the jewel have been lost under heavy piles of snow. The Giant stamps his colossal foot and an avalanche of snow falls down smothering the fool."

Arachne froze the awed listeners with an icy stare before continuing.

"Many a frozen body has been thrown off the mountain by the angry Giant. He shall let no one near his rare jewel. Perhaps, my dear, you have heard of it," Arachne taunted with a melodramatic toss of her

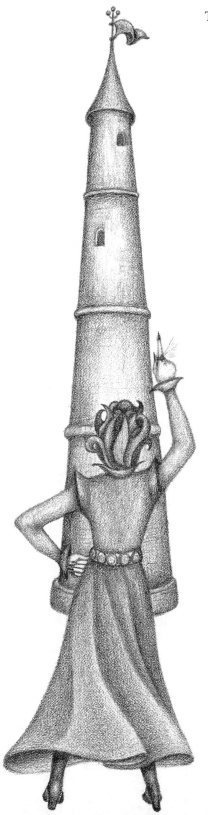

diamond covered red hair. "It is called the Green Empress!"

The crowd fluttered with excitement. Everyone in the Realm had heard of the Green Empress, the rarest emerald in the world. Anyone who possessed this gem could buy many realms.

"It is worth fortunes!" Good Fellow Sharlatan blurted out.

"Fortunes mean nothing you fool!" Arachne screamed. "The color of the Green Empress is the perfect equal of my emerald-green eyes. *That* is its *true* value!"

The crowd shuddered and fell into a terrified silence.

Satisfied that she held everyone's attention, Arachne addressed Rachel once again. "You must bring to me the Green Empress by sunrise tomorrow. And I assure you that you shall not be able to rely on your friend, Mister Elk, this time." She pointed her thin finger at the castle tower looming high over the courtyard. "You shall spend the night locked in the top of yonder tower. No elk shall reach you there!" She cackled wickedly. "Now, I must be off. I shall see you bright and early tomorrow, Rachel — the last day of your life!"

Arachne turned and climbed into the coach, slamming shut the door. The six black horses snorted and pawed the dirt restlessly. Then

44

they reared up and the coach bolted out the castle gate in a cloud of dust.

The dust made Grandy sneeze. She plucked a white hanky from her sleeve. "Arachne's the kind of woman," she sniffed, "who always wants what she can't have." She wiped her nose with the hanky. "Now I understand," she added in a whisper to Rachel, "why the King didn't want to marry her." Grandy had lost no time in catching up on the castle gossip.

"I am sorry, Rachel," said King Morland, "but you must take your place in the tower without your grandmother. I will see to it she is well provided for and we will see you at sunrise." He was again saddened that this quiet girl carried the fate of the entire Realm on her small shoulders.

Grandy and Rachel hugged each other. "I'm very frightened, Grandy," said Rachel. "Mister Elk won't be able to help me now. I don't know how I'll get to that mountain and outsmart the Giant." Rachel dropped her head down, her long dark hair hiding her eyes.

"Don't give up hope, Rachel," replied Grandy. "I would like to help you, but that would be against that spiteful woman's underhanded rules."

Rachel looked up at her grandmother. A few strands of Grandy's gray-streaked dark hair had fallen around her kind face. "Arachne called me useless," Rachel said softly.

Grandy looked into Rachel's eyes. "Those were words of fear," she said after a few moments. "You have a kind heart, and kindness is a powerful weapon against evil. Arachne is afraid of your kind heart."

Grandy smiled at Rachel, but it was a sad smile.

CHAPTER FIVE

The Green Empress

RACHEL FOLLOWED THE Royal Guard up the stairs to the top of the tower. She was locked in a room with one barred window that no elk could ever reach. She was more depressed than ever. How could she possibly solve the Second Impossible Task?

She sat down at an old wooden table in the center of the room and thought very hard, but could not come up with an answer. Many hours passed into late afternoon with Rachel no closer to solving the problem. To ease her sorrow, she began softly singing a lullaby Grandy had taught her. The melody floated through the bars of the tower window and was carried by the breeze far into the forest to Mother Bird's nest.

"I wonder — *CHIRP!* — who is singing so sadly?" said Mother Bird when she heard Rachel's lullaby. "Maybe I can help." Mother Bird flew in the direction of the melody and landed on the edge of the castle tower's window. Inside, she saw her friend. She flew

between the bars of the window and over to the table where Rachel sat, still singing softly. Rachel was looking away from the window and did not see the gentle bird.

Mother Bird cocked her head to one side. "Why are you — *CHIRP!* — singing so sadly, Rachel?" she asked.

"Oh!" exclaimed Rachel in surprise. She looked down at the table and saw her feathered friend. "I'm so glad to see you, Mother Bird! How did you find me?"

"I heard your song f l o a t i n g through the forest. It sounded — *CHIRP!* — very pretty but very sad. What is the matter?"

Rachel explained the Second Impossible Task to the kind bird. She described how the Giant jealously protected the precious emerald called the Green Empress in the far off Kingdom of Rezonantz, but somehow Rachel must have it for Arachne by sunrise tomorrow.

Mother Bird listened closely. "I think — *CHIRP!* — I can help you," she announced when Rachel had finished. "After all, you did a favor for me. You saved my little one who fell from the nest."

"But the favor I did for you was so easy," protested Rachel, "and this would be so difficult and dangerous!"

"You did for me what I could not do," replied Mother Bird. "I'll do for you what you cannot do. That's how favors are measured."

"But while you are gone who will watch your baby birds?" Rachel asked.

"Birds in the forest watch after each other's babies all the time," Mother Bird explained. "My friends are already taking care of my little ones."

"But still," Rachel objected, "how can you take such a risk?"

"If the only purpose in life — *CHIRP!* — is to avoid risk," said Mother Bird, "then life has little purpose." She winked and flew out the window, chirping a cheery tune.

Rachel was very weary from thinking. She got ready for bed and laid her head on the pillow. She tried to imagine how the tender bird could possibly capture the Green Empress, but the only thing in her mind was Mother Bird's warm, comforting voice. Soon she fell asleep and dreamed of her missing Mother.

~

Mother bird left the tower and flew as fast as she could to reach the Kingdom of Rezonantz. After several hours, she landed on the branch of a majestic fir tree on the slope of the Realm's highest mountain. It was very cold. She shivered — shaking snow from her feathered wings — then considered a plan.

"I think — *CHIRP!* — I'll fly in above the Giant," she sang. "He'll never suspect me — *CHIRP!* — he's not on the lookout for birds." She flitted up to the top branch of the tree and peered at the Giant's cottage on the peak of the mountain. Smoke rose into the clear mountain air from a crooked rock chimney on the cottage's thatched roof. Mother Bird gathered her courage and flew toward the cottage. As she got near, she could not see an open door or window to get inside. She flew in a circle around the cottage looking for an opening, but could not find one. "Oh well," she sighed, "there's only one way in." She soared high up over the roof, took a deep breath, and dove headlong down the large, smoke-filled chimney.

Through the smoke, Mother Bird saw she was zooming down into a large rock fireplace. She dodged the flames that licked at her feathers, and flew out the hearth into an immense room. A kettle the size of a bathtub filled with boiling soup hung over the large smoky blaze in the fireplace. A massive plump woman stirred the soup sluggishly. She did not notice the noiseless bird — that looked like a gray ash from the enormous fire — fly past her.

Mother Bird flew to the top of a cupboard and hid behind a large crystal bowl. The bowl was covered by a crystal lid and was filled with brightly colored pieces of candy. She preened the snow and chimney soot from her wings, then examined the room. Near the fireplace sat a long wooden table with benches on each side. At the other end of the room rested an enormous sofa. The Giant was lying on the sofa waiting for his supper.

I wonder where the Green Empress is hidden, she thought. She cocked her head and searched for a clue. *Where would I put a magnificent green emerald so that I could enjoy looking at it but no one else would find it?*

While Mother Bird scanned the room, the Giant stirred from his sleep and sat up. "When be me dinner?" he roared at the cook. His voice boomed like thunder and rattled the windows. Mother Bird's little heart skipped a beat. "What be keeping ye, ye lazy hag!" he roared again. "Me stomach's complaining!" He patted his monstrous belly and it resounded like a large kettledrum. *B A H O O M !* *BAHOOM!*

"All right! All right! It be coming," yelled the cook from the fireplace. "Leave me tend to me work. If ye cannot wait, have a piece of candy until me be ready."

The Giant grunted in a half-hearted protest. He eyed the large crystal candy bowl the gray bird was hiding

behind. Mother Bird's heart started racing. *He's coming here*, she thought. The Giant got slowly to his feet with a groan and shuffled noisily across the room toward the candy bowl. Mother Bird began to shake. A huge scabby hand came at her. Then it grabbed the lid to the candy bowl and yanked it off with a clank.

The wall-eyed Giant could focus on nothing but the candy. Mother Bird held her breath and watched. The flickering light from the fireplace danced in the etchings of the crystal and made the candies sparkle like colored stars. The Giant reached into the bowl and grabbed a piece of candy. He stuffed it into his mouth and smacked his lips. "It be mighty pretty!" his voice boomed.

That's strange, thought Mother Bird. *How could candy taste pretty?* Suddenly, her eyes lit up. *That's the clue!* she realized. *He's not talking about the candy he's eating...* Then she spotted the jewel — the emerald called the Green Empress. It was concealed by illusion — visible to the eyes yet hidden from the mind. It was right in front of Mother Bird. The emerald was in the crystal bowl filled with different colored candies. It looked like a piece of green candy. Only someone with Mother Bird's keen eyesight could have discovered it. She had found the Green Empress! *Now, how am I going to get it?* she wondered.

Just then the cook's voice screeched, "Come eat! And don't be dallying!" The Giant carelessly dropped the lid back on the bowl and lumbered over to the long table wiping his sticky hands on his coveralls. He plopped down on a bench that creaked under his weight. He grabbed a soup spoon and began sloppily sloshing the broth into his cavernous mouth.

Meanwhile, Mother Bird noticed that he had set the lid back on the candy bowl crookedly. There was an opening just big enough for her to fit through. *This is my only chance,* she thought.

While the Giant noisily slurped his soup, she flew up to the rim of the bowl. She quietly slipped through the opening and picked up the Green Empress in her beak. It was very large and difficult for her to carry. She lifted it carefully through the opening, but it was so enormous that it banged against the crystal lid. *CLINK!*

Mother Bird's heart skipped another beat.

The suspicious sound alerted the irritable cook. She came wad-dling toward the candy bowl with a dishtowel. "Hey there, ye," she yelled, "what be ye doing?" Mother Bird flew into the air carrying the large emerald in her beak. The cook snapped at the bird with the dishtowel. "Gimme that!" she cried. Mother Bird flitted just out of range of the snapping towel, still holding the Green Empress firmly.

Then the moody Giant rose awkwardly from his bench — still holding his soup spoon — and stumbled after the cook. "Try to steal me Green Empress, will ye! We'll see about that!" He joined in the chase, swinging the soup spoon — which still had soup in it — in the air. It made quite a mess splashing the thick broth on everything — even on the Green Empress.

Mother Bird flew around the room for several minutes dodging the spoon and the towel. The Giant and the cook scrambled after her in a frenzy — banging into everything in the room in a rumbling, bumbling, fumbling spectacle. Mother Bird soon grew tired. She knew she had to come up with a plan before she dropped out of the air from exhaustion. *Maybe I should face the problem head on*, she thought. And that was her plan!

The Giant and the Cook chase Mother Bird.

Mother Bird flew to the other side of the room — as far away from the Giant as she could get. Then she turned and rocketed straight at the over-sized ogre's surprised face! When she was so close she could peck his huge nose, she swooped down and flew between his towering legs.

The clumsy Giant foolishly bent over to catch the bird between his legs, but the cook — who was still looking up in the air — ran backwards into his behind and they both fell into a twisted pile on the floor with a t h u n d e r i n g crash.

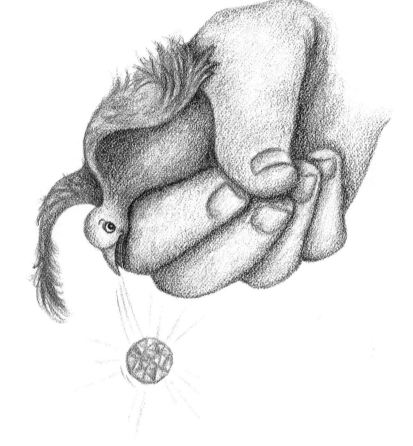

FARUMPH! As the enraged Giant scrambled to get up, Mother Bird raced toward the fireplace.

The plan worked! she thought. But just as she started up the hot chimney, a huge hand grabbed hold of her tail feathers. "Now me's got ye!" roared the Giant. Instantly, Mother Bird let loose of the soup-covered Green Empress, which started falling into the fire. As the Giant grabbed for the slick emerald, Mother Bird slipped out of his gnarled hand. The Giant caught the Green Empress, but as the flames licked at his leathery fingers, he let out an ear-shattering yell — "YEEOWW!" — and dropped it again.

Mother Bird dove through the flame and caught the jewel in her beak. She shot up the chimney and out into the freezing mountain air, her singed feathers trailing a wisp of smoke. She fluttered to a nearby tree to hide and catch her breath.

The growling Giant came crashing through the cottage door after her. "Where be that thief of a bird?" he roared at the cook who trundled along behind him in the fresh snow.

"When me look for birds," the cook answered, "me look up." Her breath puffed white fluffy clouds in the icy night air.

The Giant squinted up into the dark sky. He saw nothing but shining silver stars and a cold moon.

"Methinks ye lost the Green Empress," said the cook. "She be pretty," she added dryly, "but she did not cook ye soup."

"AAARRRGGGHHH!" roared the Giant in anger. He began jumping up and down in the snow. The mountain began to echo and tremble. *AHH-WOOO-AHH! AHH-WOOO-AHH! AHH-WOOO-AHH!* Suddenly, a huge avalanche of snow came crashing down on top of both the Giant and his cook. *WOOOMMFF! WOOOMMFF! WOMMMPPP!*

The avalanche just missed Mother Bird's tree, but the blast engulfed her in a misty white cloud of ice and snow, and almost knocked her off her perch. The Green Empress fell into a deep snow bank beneath the tree. "Oh, my," she chirped.

After the air cleared, she examined her feathers. They were singed, soupy, sooty, snowy, and sleety — not in good shape for a long distance flight. And flying with the Green Empress in her beak would make the long trip back to Rachel even more difficult. *Even if I find the lost jewel,* she worried, *I don't know if I can reach the castle before sunrise. I will have to fly as hard as I can and hope the winds do their part to help.* She swooped down beneath the tree and began pecking for the green emerald in the white snow.

~

EARLY NEXT MORNING, Rachel awoke with a start. She looked around the room, but didn't see Mother Bird or the Green Empress. She became quite concerned and jumped out of bed. She searched anxiously, but couldn't find the emerald. Her heart began to beat faster. *Mother Bird wasn't able to get the Green Empress, after all,* she guessed. *I do hope nothing happened to her.* Somberly, Rachel began to get ready to face Arachne. She was so worried about Mother Bird, she didn't notice any-

thing in her shoe when she picked it up. "Ouch!" she squealed as she tried to slip the shoe on her foot. She pulled the shoe off to find the cause of the irritation. She turned it over and out onto the bed fell a spattered stone.

Still worrying about Mother Bird, Rachel absent-mindedly

picked the dirty stone off the bed and started to wipe it with a hand towel. As she cleaned the stone, it began to cast a wondrous green glow. Rachel looked more closely at the curious object. "This is the Green Empress!" she suddenly cried out. "Mother Bird must have dropped it in my shoe so I'd be sure to find it. This means she's okay!" Rachel breathed a sigh of relief. *I wonder how the Green Empress got so dirty*, she thought. *I must clean it so Arachne won't be angry.* A mischievous smile crossed her lips.

When Rachel finished polishing the Green Empress, she realized she was hungry. She ate the small breakfast the Royal Guard had set on the table. Soon there was a knock on the door and Rachel skipped across the room just as it opened. Good King Morland stood at the door, bent and sad. "I am sorry, Rachel, but it is almost sunrise," he said. "We must meet Arachne in the courtyard. This is very difficult."

"I believe more difficult for Arachne, Your Majesty, than for us," exclaimed Rachel. She held out her hand and showed the King the magnificent polished emerald.

"You have done it again!" the King shouted. He let out a hardy laugh and started to dance. Rachel, too, began dancing.

Soon, Grandy came into the room, puffing from her climb up the tower stairs. "What's going on?" she asked. She was startled to see the King and Rachel laughing and dancing all around.

"Rachel has done it!" exclaimed the King.

"Wait until Arachne sees this," said Rachel. She showed Grandy the luminous Green Empress.

"She will be furious!" all three of them shouted at once.

Rachel quickly finished getting ready and the happy trio hurried down the tower steps to join Queen Allandra and the people of the Realm in the castle courtyard. They all gasped in disbelief when they saw Rachel holding the Green Empress.

Good Fellow Sharlatan cleared his throat — "Ahem" — and then spoke up. "I believe she's done it again," he announced. The crowd began to murmur excitedly.

Rachel and King Morland dance.

Then, just at sunrise, the frightful black coach raced through the castle gate and came to a shuddering stop. Everyone fell silent. Arachne stepped from the coach and glared at Rachel in defiance. She wore a stunning emerald-green gown to match her eyes.

"Do not expect me to believe you have the Green Empress," she said, holding out her hand sarcastically.

"You don't have to believe me," said Rachel. "You can believe the Green Empress herself." She stepped forward and carefully placed the magnificent emerald in Arachne's white hand.

Arachne's emerald-green eyes grew wide as she gazed at the jewel. It was precisely the color she saw each time she peered at her eyes in

her looking glass. Then her face slowly turned red with fury.

"Well," she said, glaring at Rachel, "you have done it again. You captured the Green Empress. Two times you have beaten me — the all-powerful Arachne — when no one else has triumphed over me even once. I know that your friend the elk did not help you." She impatiently stamped her foot on the step of the coach, her emerald-green gown shimmering in the morning sunlight. "So what is your story today?"

"My friend Mother Bird…" Rachel began politely.

"A bird!" screeched Arachne.

Rachel ignored the outburst and continued. "...was kind enough to help me. Like Mister Elk, I did a favor for her and she wanted to repay the kindness." Her voice was soft but did not shake like before. Her fear of this evil woman was turning to something else. She almost felt pity for Arachne, who seemed to act like a very lonely person.

"The Second Impossible Task was for the birds!" Grandy shouted at Arachne. The crowd laughed.

Arachne glared at Grandy. "Who is this vile creature?" she demanded with a sneer.

"She is a very loyal resident of the Realm," answered Queen Allandra before anyone else could speak.

"I'm a loyal resident and a royal pain," added Grandy. Everyone laughed again — even the King and Queen.

Arachne huffed and turned her venomous look on Rachel. *How can this ragamuffin keep succeeding in these tasks?* she thought. *I shall give her a truly impossible task today. I shall not lose this game.* "Very well," she said. "You have twice beaten me, but you shall never gain a third victory." She paused, still glaring at Rachel. Then she continued in an icy, ruthless voice.

"Here is the Third Impossible Task. In the far off Sea of Lusenta, at the bottom of the ocean, lies a black pearl necklace — the only one of its kind. It belongs to the Princess of the Mermaids. The Sea of Lusenta is guarded by a monstrous red dragon. The dragon has one eye at the top of its head, so it sees in all directions at once. You shall not catch the dragon unaware, because it never sleeps. And perchance you should slip past the dragon, you should not take hope. The Sea of Lusenta is surrounded by high jagged rocks which are impossible to cross. And if you somehow traverse the rocks, your dangers have just begun. You must swim to the bottom of the Sea of Lusenta, which is filled with hungry sharks. They would find you quite tasty."

Arachne paused to watch the terrified crowd's reaction to her biting remarks. With a thin smile of satisfaction she continued.

"And if the sharks would not have you, the giant spring clams — with powerful shells that snap open in an instant — would enjoy a pretty little snack. A spring clam can trap a whole shark in its shell. If perchance you should elude the sharks and giant spring clams, your pathetic adventure would be for naught. The black pearl necklace is so cleverly hidden that you would surely drown — horribly, I might add — before you discovered it. No one has ever attempted this task — even the bravest knights tremble with fear just thinking about the black pearl necklace." A devious smirk came over Arachne's face. "Black, of course, goes so well with my eyes," she concluded with a flicker of her emerald-green eyes.

The crowd trembled. Arachne was sure Rachel would fail this time. Rachel was sure she would fail this time too. Even Grandy was sure Rachel would fail this time. Queen Allandra's eyes grew moist.

Arachne burst into a laugh when she saw the sea of sad faces. "Tonight, you flippant child, you shall be placed in a dank cell at the bottom of the dungeon where neither your elk friend nor your bird friend can help you. There are no windows!" Then she turned her vengeful gaze on the King. "Well, Your Royal Majesty, it appears I shall win this game yet!"

Arachne climbed into the coach. Instantly the horses reared up and charged toward the castle gate. Arachne waved her spidery hand mockingly from the window. "By the way," she called to the King and Queen, "I notice the Royal Garden is filthy with flies. Who *ever* will you find to get rid of them?"

"Flies!" Grandy shouted, hugging Rachel, "that witch has flies buzzing in her head. It seems she's going to destroy not only the Royal Garden, but the entire Realm along with my granddaughter."

The King, the Queen and the people of the Realm were disheartened. The day no longer looked so bright. No one knew what to do. "We are in quite a fix," observed Good Fellow Sharlatan.

"I don't see how anyone could succeed at the Third Impossible Task," agreed Rachel. "I'm afraid it's hopeless."

CHAPTER SIX

The Black Pearls

THE ROYAL GUARDS led Rachel down the dark winding stairs to the dungeon. At the bottom of the stairs, they crossed a rickety bridge over a trickling stream that ran under the castle walls and past a cell made of iron bars. Rachel's shadow danced eerily in the flickering light of burning torches mounted on the mossy rock walls. The dungeon had no windows.

The Royal Guards locked Rachel in the cell with a loud clank. She looked around. The cell seemed like a large cage. It was gloomy and damp, although the Royal Guards had tried to make it as nice as possible for her. The creaky old bed had clean linen. And they had placed a candle and a small lunch on the wobbly wooden table in the center of the cell. The table had one wooden chair.

Rachel was not hungry, but she sat on the hard chair

and took a few bites of food, hoping the nourishment would help her mind come up with a plan. She felt terrible. Surely she would fail now without her friends, Mother Bird and Mister Elk. *But I must not give up,* she thought. *Maybe I can come up with a plan.*

The food made Rachel thirsty. She took the tin cup from her kerchief and tried to reach through the iron bars to get water from the stream. But she did not put her heart into it and could not reach the water. She pulled the cup back and it accidentally banged against one of the bars. *CLANG!* She listened to the curious sound, then tried a different bar. *CLING! These are musical bars,* she thought.

To pass the time while she planned, she began playing a song by clinking her cup on the bars of the cell. *CLING! CLANG! CLONG!* She did not realize that the sounds echoed off the dungeon wall into the stream and were carried through the water into the creeks and ponds of the Royal Forest.

The sound reached the reflecting pond, causing ripples across the surface. "A rippled surface — surface rippled," said Captain Toad. "Ripples cannot reflect — reflect cannot ripples."

He quickly swam up the stream to see what was creating the disturbance. He followed the stream under the castle wall and jumped out of the water when he got to the dungeon. He hopped through the bars of the cell sprinkling water everywhere. Rachel had shut her eyes to think and did not see the toad until she felt the spray of water in her face.

"Oh my," she squealed, opening her eyes.

"What is this — this is what?" croaked Captain Toad. "Need some help — help some need?"

Rachel burst into a smile when she saw her funny friend. "Oh, Captain Toad, I'm so happy to see you, but I don't think anyone can help me."

"Let me be the judge — judge be me," he admonished.

Rachel described the Third Impossible Task. She told him about the precious black pearl necklace that belonged to the Mermaid Princess in the Sea of Lusenta, and about the one-eyed dragon and the hun-

Rachel plays musical bars with her tin cup.

gry sharks and giant spring clams and all the events that landed her in the underground cell.

Captain Toad listened intensely, his eyes getting bigger and bigger. When she finished, he clicked his tongue. *CLICK! CLICK!*

That doesn't sound good, thought Rachel.

"Think I can help — help can I think," the toad finally said. He jumped in the air and almost hit his wet brown head on the dank ceiling. "Water creatures know the Mermaid Princess — Princess Mermaid know," he explained. "One black pearl necklace coming up — up coming necklace pearl black." And before Rachel could speak, Captain Toad hopped back into the stream and splashed away.

I didn't know toads were that brave, Rachel thought. *Maybe he didn't understand how dangerous it would be — he doesn't always seem to listen.* But deep in her heart there glimmered a spark of hope for her future.

She finished the lunch on the table and, by stretching a little farther than she had before, was able to fill her cup with water from the stream.

Queen Allandra had kindly left a nightgown, a wash cloth and pail of warm sudsy water in the cell. Rachel washed herself, then put on the nightgown and spent the afternoon washing her clothes and hanging them to dry. She tried to be brave but by bedtime she felt Captain Toad was not going to make it. She couldn't imagine how the lighthearted toad could survive the ruthless dragon and all the other dangers of the Third Impossible Task. As her spirits dimmed, she hoped only that the funny toad would not be hurt attempting this brave deed. She fell into a troubled sleep and began dreaming about her funny lost brother Tod.

~

WHEN CAPTAIN TOAD left Rachel, he swam close to the muddy bottom of the stream to avoid the alligators guarding the castle. He was soon covered with mud himself. He knew the waterways well and did not get lost as he took the many turns to reach the far off Sea of Lusenta. But as afternoon turned to evening, it became so dark underwater that he began bumping into rocks. Suddenly one of the rocks opened its big mouth showing rows of jagged teeth.

"Oops-a-daisy — daisy-oops!" sputtered Captain Toad, "No rock that — that rock no!" He paddled his powerful legs, racing to the surface as fast as he could and splashed out of the stream just as the jaws of a bad-tempered alligator crashed down behind him. *CRUNCH!*

Captain Toad sprang out of the way and leaped to the safety of a high rock. He shook off the mud and water and looked to see if he still had both his legs. He did. "No toad's legs today — today legs toad's no!" he yelled at the angry alligator. The gator was not amused and slipped sullenly back into the murky stream.

"Getting late — late getting," Captain Toad croaked. The water dripping off him formed a puddle on the rock that seemed strangely red in the setting sun. "Time to hustle — hustle to time." He crouched into a springing position to jump from the rock into the stream. Suddenly the rock started to move.

"Land tremor — tremor land," he sputtered. He looked down and saw he was not on a rock at all, but on the red snout of the monstrous one-eyed dragon! He turned around and saw the large bloodshot eye staring at him. "Yipes! I must be near the Sea of Lusenta — Lusenta Sea near be," he said to the puzzled dragon. The monster's nostrils started to spew steam. *HISSSSSSSS!* And a roar came rumbling up from deep inside its gigantic scaly body. "RRRAAAHHHRRR!"

"Look, leap, lick — lick, leap, look!" cried Captain Toad. Then he leaped high in the air — *SPROING!* — and zapped the dragon in the eye with his lightning-fast tongue. *ZZZBLAT!*

The furious dragon whipped its powerful tail over the top of its head. The tail missed Captain Toad by inches and, instead, came crashing across the dragon's own snout — *CARRRUNCH!* — where Captain Toad had just been perched. The battered monster let out another ear-

shattering roar — "RRRAAAHHHRRR!" — followed by a huge ball of fire. *WHOOOFFF!*

The ball of fire caught Captain Toad in mid-leap and sent him tumbling through the scorching air. He landed in a mound of soft mud next to the stream — *SPLOIT!* — where his charred body cooled in the wet ooze. *PSSSHHH!* The sightless dragon swung its tail again in a blind rage, but Captain Toad hopped up out of the way — *BOING!* — just as the tail swooped beneath him and knocked over a tree. *KAAABOSH!*

Captain Toad landed back in the cool mud and ana-lyzed his sticky predicament. The dragon could not see out of its huge watery eye, so Cap-tain Toad was safe as long as he made no noise. But behind the dragon rose the high, jagged rocks surrounding the Sea of Lusenta. Even if he could sneak past the dragon, he did not know how he could ever get over the dangerous rocks.

Just then the dragon's tail swished back toward him. He hopped up in the nick of time — *BOING!* — and the tail swooped harmlessly under his feet and knocked over an-other tree. *KAAABOSH!* Cap-tain Toad landed again in the mud — but this time he came down with an idea.

"Yoo hoo — hoo yoo!" he called to the dragon in a friendly voice. "Let's be pals — pals be let's."

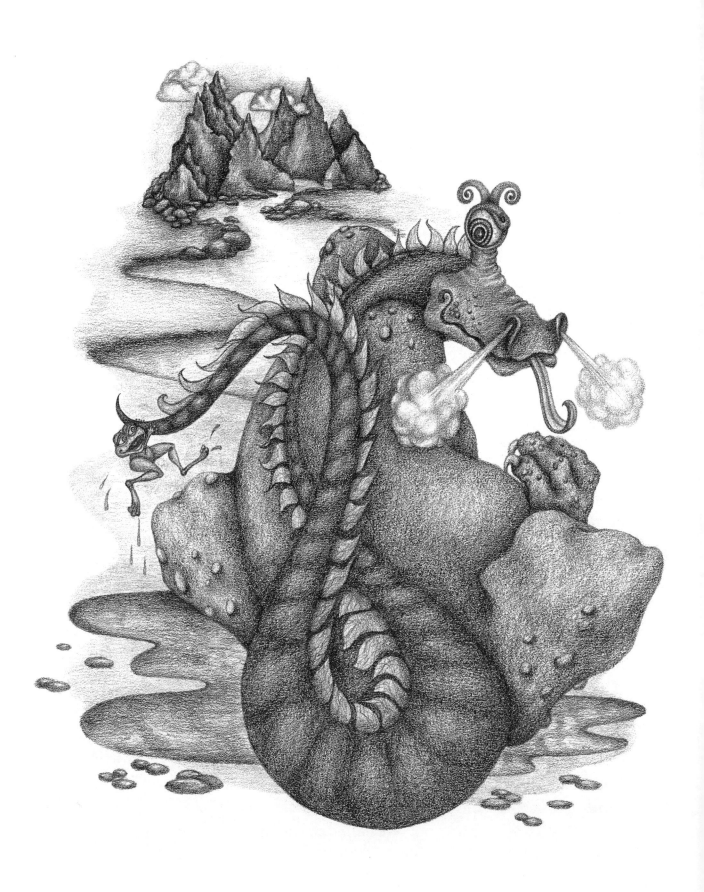

Captain Toad rides on the Dragon's tail.

As expected, the outraged dragon swung its huge tail in the direction of the toad. Again, Captain Toad hopped up — *BOING!* — but instead of landing back in the mud, he came down on top of the lethal tail as it swept under him. The massive tail just missed several trees and whipped high into the air with Captain Toad hanging onto the tip for dear life.

When the tail reached full height, he sprang off the end and soared like a missile into the purple evening sky, sailing safely over the towering jagged rocks and landing with a big splash in the legendary Sea of Lusenta — which, he suddenly remembered, was infested with toad-eating sharks.

According to toad experts, sharks attack swimmers on the surface of the water, so Captain Toad dove for the bottom of the ocean where he immediately came face to face with a shark that did not believe in toad experts. Before the surprised shark could open its mouth to have a toad supper, Captain Toad cocked his powerful legs and bopped the hungry fish on the nose with his feet. *PRONG!*

The stunned shark turned and swam away. Captain Toad knew that no self-respecting killer likes to be bopped on the nose and, like most bullies, they run away when someone bangs them on the snout. What Captain Toad forgot was that

this particular shark did not play by the rules. Suddenly, the enraged shark turned back and came charging at the toad with revenge in its beady eyes.

Captain Toad gulped. "GLUB — GLUB!" Then he shot through the water as fast as his churning legs could take him, the ill-humored shark close on his tail. The chase continued with the shark getting ever closer until Captain Toad spied an opening in an underwater rock formation. He spurted through the opening just as the shark clamped its jaws. CR*UMP!* But the opening was not quite large enough for the shark. The killer fish jammed to a halt halfway through the rocks. *SCREECH!*

"Toodle-loo — loo-toodle," Captain Toad called to the shark. He turned to swim away, but banged right into the open shell of a giant spring clam. He dodged out of the way just as the shell snapped shut. *CLAMP!* "And toodle-loo to you too — too you to loo-toodle," he called to the gigantic clam, and swam away.

Nighttime had fallen on the Sea of Lusenta, but the water had a ghostly green glow. This was just enough light for Captain Toad to navigate to the under-sea bedchamber of the famous Mermaid Princess. He arrived as the Mermaid Princess was getting ready for a big night of dancing at the social event of the season — Neptune's Annual Beach Ball.

The bedchamber was truly a dazzling sight. The bed was a gigantic pearly oyster shell under a canopy of glistening jewels. Fresh green seaweed served as curtains, and the Mermaid Princess herself sat at a beautiful coral pink dressing table in front of a large looking glass. A bevy of mermaid handmaidens scurried around tidying the bedchamber and tending to the Mermaid Princess. Captain Toad hid behind a seaweed curtain and watched.

"Oh, Your Majesty," said one of her handmaidens. "You will be the most beautiful mermaid at Neptune's Beach Ball tonight!" The handmaiden gently brushed the long green hair of the Mermaid Princess with a comb made of shark's teeth.

"Yes, Star, you are quite correct," sniffed the Mermaid Princess. "I am beautiful."

Captain Toad sees the bedchamber of the Mermaid Princess.

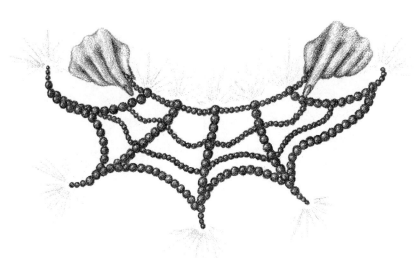

She sure is stuck on herself — herself on stuck, thought Captain Toad.

The Mermaid Princess admired herself in the looking glass. "I shall wear my black pearl necklace," she instructed Star. "Please get it for me." Except for the Mermaid Princess, only Star knew where the precious black pearl necklace was hidden. "The others shall leave me now," the Mermaid Princess said as she waved her pale green hand in dismissal.

The handmaidens quickly glided out of the bedchamber, their tales swishing back and forth in harmony like flowers blowing in the breeze. Then, Star swam to the oyster-shell bed

76

and reached beneath it. She grabbed an ordinary looking conch shell and pulled from it the wonderful black pearl necklace. Captain Toad's eyes bulged with amazement at the sight of the shiny black pearls. He watched Star place the necklace around the pale, delicate neck of the Mermaid Princess.

"Exquisite!" said the Mermaid Princess, still regarding her image in the looking glass. "The black pearls look so nice next to my lovely neck." Star agreed most heartily. "I shall return at midnight, Star," the Princess continued, rising from her seat. "Be certain to have my night things ready for me when I get home. I will be tired from dancing with all the sea kings at the Beach Ball." She wafted gracefully out of the bedchamber like a delicate leaf in a gentle breeze and slipped smoothly into her carriage, which was a large sand dollar pulled by twenty strong seahorses. Away they churned.

Captain Toad was worried. The Mermaid Princess would not return with the black pearl necklace until midnight. It would be put back in the conch shell and the conch shell would be placed under the bed. The problem was that according to legend there were ten thousand shells under the bed of the Mermaid Princess. How would he know which shell held the necklace unless he had a clue?

As he tried to puzzle out this problem, he kept thinking about the handmaiden named Star. Except for the Mermaid Princess, only Star

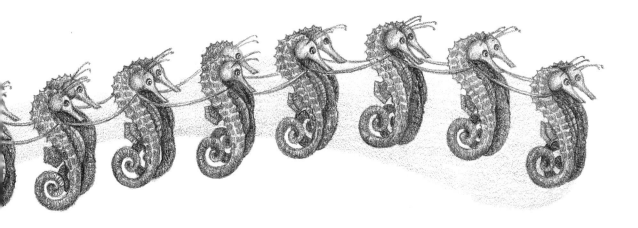

knew which shell held the necklace. *Why Star — Star why?* he thought. *Star light — light Star. Star bright — bright Star.* Just then a fish wandered through the bedchamber. *Fish Star — Star fish. That is it — it is that!* Captain Toad suddenly realized. The tired toad had his clue and immediately fell asleep.

The whinnying of seahorses woke him several hours later. The Mermaid Princess was returning from Neptune's Beach Ball in her sand dollar carriage. As the carriage bubbled to a stop, the Mermaid Princess nimbly eased out of it with a delicate yawn. Captain Toad rubbed his eyes and saw that she still wore the black pearl necklace. T*ake it off — off it take!* he wanted to yell. But he didn't make a sound from his hiding place behind the seaweed curtain.

"Star, where are you?" called the Mermaid Princess. Her green hair swirled around her. "I am ready for you now. I am so tired." Star appeared with the Mermaid Princess's night things.

"Did you have a grand time, Your Majesty?" asked Star as she helped the Mermaid Princess get into her nightgown.

"I was the belle of the Beach Ball," bragged the Mermaid Princess. "Everyone there was jealous of my beauty and the black pearl necklace." She carefully took off the necklace and held it up in front of her. "It really is the most beautiful necklace in the world." Then she handed it to Star. "Please put it away now. It is time to sleep." She climbed into the large oyster-shell bed and fell fast asleep. Star dropped the necklace into the conch shell and placed the shell out of sight far beneath the bed.

When Star left the room, Captain Toad swam over to the bed and peered underneath. He saw thousands of shells and a large purple starfish. It would have been impossible to find the right shell without a clue. But he had a clue. Each of the five arms of the starfish pointed to a different shell.

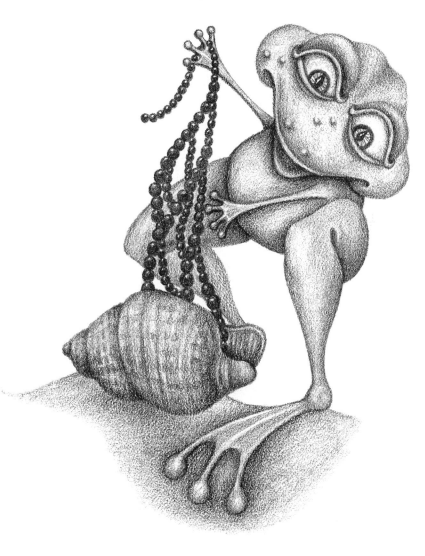

Captain Toad picked up the first shell and looked inside, but found nothing. He looked in the second, third, and fourth shells — all empty. The fifth shell was empty too. *Red herrings — herrings red*, thought Captain Toad. But he did not give up. He raised up the starfish. Underneath, he found a single conch shell. *Hope this is it — it is this hope!* He reached inside the shell and pulled out the precious black pearl necklace!

He quickly curled the necklace into his long tongue and stored it safely in his mouth. Just then the Mermaid Princess moaned in her sleep. Captain Toad raced out of her chambers and began swimming along the ocean floor with all his might toward the castle.

It was very late and he didn't know if he could get to Rachel's cell in the dungeon before sunrise. He still had to get past the sharks and giant spring clams, the jagged rocks, the dragon, and the alligators. His toad heart was beating wildly.

Captain Toad swam hard and made it safely to the shallow water near the edge of the Sea of Lusenta without seeing any sharks. He was quietly swimming among a bed of giant spring clams — taking care not to make any noise that would cause the powerful shells to spring open.

Suddenly he saw the ill-natured shark he had banged on the nose earlier. It was coming toward him at full speed — there was no time to get away!

Captain Toad had to think quickly — and in an instant he had a plan. He drifted casually to the rear of a spring clam's closed shell as the shark closed in on him. He gave the killer fish a friendly wave, further infuriating it.

When the shark was three seconds away, Captain Toad calmly knocked on the giant spring clam's shell. *KNOCK! KNOCK!* When the shark was two seconds away, Captain Toad called out to the spring clam in a neighborly voice. "Is anybody home — home anybody?" And just one second before the hurtling shark crushed Captain Toad in its powerful jaws, the colossal clam shell snapped open in the shark's face. *WHOOSH!*

Instead of grabbing Captain Toad, the shark smashed headlong into the open shell — *CLUNK!* — which instantly closed, leaving nothing but a wriggling shark tail hanging out. "Breakfast in bed — bed in breakfast," Captain Toad called to the giant spring clam as he swam away.

When Captain Toad reached the seashore, he wondered how he was going to get back over the jagged rocks surrounding the Sea of Lusenta. They were too slippery and steep to climb. Maybe he could leap over them. *It would take a super jump — jump super take,* he thought. But he was too worn out from swimming to try such a leap. Then an idea occurred to him.

He swam over to the nearest giant spring clam whose shell would open toward the rocks and climbed on top of the closed shell. "Here goes nothing — nothing goes," he said, and knocked on the shell. *KNOCK!* Nothing happened. He knocked again. *KNOCK! KNOCK!* Still nothing happened. He knocked a third time. *KNOCK! KNOCK! KNOCK!* Suddenly, the powerful shell snapped open in a cloud of sea bubbles. *WHOOSH!* It sent Captain Toad flying high into the early morning sky

— clean over the top of the jagged rocks surrounding the Sea of Lusenta.

He plummeted down on the other side, landing on the snout of the blinded dragon — *BOP!* — who was still bellowing and knocking trees down with his tail. *CRASH! BANG! BOOM!* "Good morning — morning good," he said to the dragon. Then he leaped from the snout, bounced over some fallen trees — *BOING!* — and plunged into the stream — *KERRRSPLASH!* — just ahead of the dragon's tail. *SWISH!*

Captain Toad swam toward the castle, but he was completely worn out from his adventure. *No quitting now — now quitting no,* he determined. At that moment he felt something powerful clamp around his foot. He looked around and was eye-to-eye with a hungry alligator. "Oops-a-daisy — daisy-oops!" he said. "This could be serious — serious could be." He decided he needed yet another plan.

He smiled at the surprised alligator and spread his arms invitingly. "Why not take all of me — me all take?" he taunted. This was too much for the greedy gator. It opened its huge jaws to gobble up the whole toad, but Captain Toad pulled his foot free and shot out of reach just as the mouth banged shut. *CHOMP!*

Meanwhile, the black pearl necklace had fallen out of Captain Toad's mouth. He dived toward the muddy bottom of the stream to find it, with the chomping gator close behind. As he reached bottom he stepped nimbly to one side. The pursuing gator missed the turn and slammed headlong into the slime. *GLOP!* The gator's tail thrashed back and forth as it tried to pull its front end out of the goop. "Stuck in the mud, are we — we are mud stuck?" said Captain Toad to the alligator. The gator's reply — *GURGLE!* — was not clear.

It was now getting very late and the castle was still very far away. Captain Toad was exhausted and the necklace was lost somewhere in the murky bottom of the stream. He let out a sigh. "Glug! — glug!" Then he began frantically rummaging through the brown mud for the black pearl necklace.

~

BACK AT THE CASTLE, Rachel did not sleep well during the night. She worried about her friend, Captain Toad. The dungeon had no windows but as the hours passed by she knew it must nearly be dawn — Captain Toad had been gone for such a long time. Her heart sank. "I didn't think he'd be able to do it," she sighed.

She was very sad. She sat up in the bed and looked at the cold stream through the bars of the cell. As she watched, a strange ball of mud slowly emerged out of the water. She gasped. Suddenly the ball of mud sprouted two eyes. *POP! POP!* Then it jiggled, spraying a misty brown cloud of mud and water that hid the weird creature. When the cloud cleared, Rachel's eyes almost popped out of her own head. It was not a ball of mud at all — it was Captain Toad!

"Captain Toad," she cried, "I'm so happy you're back!" She did not see the black pearl necklace. "Don't worry about that silly black pearl necklace. Nobody could have gotten it. I'm just glad you're all right."

Captain Toad did not speak, but he sloshed slowly over to the cell and through the bars. *SSSLOP!*

SSSLOP! SSSLOP! His tired mouth fell open and the long tongue un-rolled in front of Rachel.

"Oops-a-daisy!" said Rachel, jumping backwards. Then she saw it! Dangling at the end of Captain Toad's out-stretched tongue dangled the black pearl necklace! "Oh, Captain Toad," she shouted, "you've saved the Realm!"

Before Rachel could thank him, Captain Toad tossed the necklace on the bed without a word and sloshed back to the stream. His limp body fell into the water — *KERPLUNK!* — and disappeared.

I guess there was nothing to say, Rachel thought. "Thank you..." she said sadly to the ripple in the stream where Captain Toad had just vanished. Then — remembering with a tear in her eye the reflective way her happy-go-lucky friend talked — she added softly, "...you thank!"

Rachel feared she would never see Captain Toad again.

CHAPTER SEVEN

Three Magic Wishes

RACHEL BEGAN GETTING ready to meet Arachne. She untangled her hair with a comb Queen Allandra had left in the cell, washed her face in a basin of water by her bed, and slipped into the clean frock that had dried overnight. Then she put on her bonnet and blue cape. When she had finished, she sat on the bed and polished the black pearls with a wash cloth. She thought about Captain Toad, Mother Bird, and Mister Elk. She would surely miss her friends. She sniffed back another tear.

"Rachel!" a happy voice suddenly rang out. "You have the black pearl necklace!"

Rachel looked up and saw Queen Allandra standing outside the bars of the cell. "Good morning, Your Highness," she said, hopping to her feet.

"This is wonderful!" cried the Queen. "We were all so worried."

"My friend Captain Toad was very brave," said Rachel. "He brought the black pearls to me only a few minutes ago. He was quite exhausted by the adventure."

"But why do you look so sad?" asked the Queen.

"I'm afraid I'll never again see my animal friends — Captain Toad, Mother Bird, and Mister Elk," Rachel explained.

"I see," said Queen Allandra. "You will have to excuse me for now. The Royal Guards will be here soon to take you to see Arachne one last time." Then the Queen quickly crossed the rickety bridge over the stream and hurried up the stairs out of the dungeon.

Rachel waited. It seemed like an eternity before the Royal Guards appeared at the iron bars of her cell. The King and Queen were not with them. Grandy was not with them either.

"Is Arachne here yet?" asked Rachel.

"No, miss," answered one of the Royal Guards unlocking the cell door. "But we must hurry, it is almost sunrise."

Rachel followed the Royal Guards up the stairs and out of the dungeon. The largest crowd ever had gathered in the courtyard. They broke into a loud cheer when Rachel stepped into the pre-dawn light — and the cheer turned to a thundering roar when they saw the black pearl necklace in her hand.

Rachel looked around, but could not see the King or the Queen or Grandy. *Where could they be?* she wondered. But her thoughts were interrupted.

"Rachel saved the Realm!" shouted Good Fellow Sharlatan. Then the whole crowd began chanting. "Rachel! Rachel! Rachel!"

The crowd continued chanting until Arachne's black coach rumbled into the courtyard and stopped in front of the unpretentious girl in blue. The onlookers grew still in eager anticipation. Arachne got out and stood disdainfully on the coach step as usual. She wore a gossamer silver crown — with diamonds that sparkled like dew drops — in her blazing red hair. She was dressed in a lavish black velvet gown with a matching belt around her waist. The belt clasp in the center of

86

her stomach was a large blood-red ruby.

The sight was more dazzling and strange than anything Rachel could ever imagine — she remembered a black widow spider with a red mark on its belly that had frightened her once many years ago. Arachne smiled thinly and scanned the deathly quiet crowd. She was quite sure she had won.

Suddenly her emerald-green eyes caught sight of the black pearl necklace in Rachel's hand. Arachne shuddered. She quickly reached down and snatched the glistening necklace. She gazed at the string of black pearls in disbelief, then furiously draped it around her neck. It looked beautiful — but Arachne's face was cold and bitter.

"Just how did you manage this!" Arachne screamed at Rachel in a desperate voice.

"My friend Captain Toad…" Rachel began.

Arachne looked aghast. "A toad!" she interrupted sharply. "Impossible! Toads are good for nothing but catching flies — the most *disgusting* practice on the face of the earth!" Arachne twisted her face in horror and revulsion at the thought of catching flies. Her emerald-green eyes flickered with hatred.

At that moment, King Morland, Queen Allandra, and Grandy came walking into the courtyard from the castle gate. A happy smile crossed Rachel's face when she first saw them coming toward her.

The King, Queen and Grandy with Rachel's animal friends.

Then she looked again. Walking next to the King was a large ant-lered animal — it was Mister Elk! And on Queen Allandra's shoulder perched a gentle gray bird — it was Mother Bird! And a wet brown amphibian sat merrily on top of Grandy's head — it was Captain Toad!

Rachel clapped her hands and jumped up and down laughing. "Mister Elk! Mother Bird! Captain Toad!" she called out.

Arachne looked with panic at the three animals coming toward her. "THESE CANNOT BE THE CREATURES THAT HELPED YOU!" she screamed hysterically at Rachel. She blinked her emerald-green eyes in disbelief. Her face seemed wild like that of a frightened animal. "THEY ARE MY OWN CREATIONS!"

Rachel did not understand what Arachne meant.

"Do these critters give you jitters?" Grandy yelled at Arachne when they arrived at the coach. The crowd laughed and cheered Grandy.

"How did my friends get here?" Rachel asked the King.

"Queen Allandra told Grandy and me how Captain Toad helped you capture the black pearl necklace," explained King Morland, "and that you were afraid you would never again see your animal friends. So we sent the Royal Army out into the forest early this morning to find Captain Toad, Mother Bird, and Mister Elk." The King smiled at the three animals. "The Queen and I had waited outside the castle gate with Grandy until the helpful animals arrived, just now."

Arachne was horrified. She realized she had lost the challenge. She desperately jumped into the coach and tried to escape. But Mister Elk leaped in front of the horses before they could move. Meanwhile, Captain Toad jumped in the coach window and licked Arachne's ear with his long tongue. Arachne let out a blood-curdling scream and jumped out of the coach with a terrified look on her face. Mother Bird then flew over to Arachne and tugged on the black pearl necklace, pull-ing her over to the King and Queen.

"Well, Arachne," said King Morland, "you are defeated and have lost your powers."

Arachne bowed her head. "Not quite," she said softly. "I must grant Three Magic Wishes to the person who performed the Three Impossible Tasks. After that my powers are lost forever."

All eyes turned to Rachel. The young girl's eyes grew wide.

"What are your Three Magic Wishes?"

Arachne asked Rachel.

"Three Magic Wishes?" Rachel said uncertainly.

"Please," Arachne begged — her emerald-green eyes glimmering.

Rachel looked up at the King and Queen. "I wish that every tree and flower, every fruit and vegetable, and everything that grows in the Royal Garden and throughout the Realm could be once again fresh and beautiful."

Arachne covered her emerald-green eyes with her hands and chanted, "Spin, magic, spin!" Then she thrust her hands up in the air and tiny filaments of silken thread spun skyward from each finger creating a spidery web that instantly blanketed the entire Realm.

Immediately the Royal Garden and the entire Realm burst forth with lush plants and trees — fuller, richer and more fragrant and beautiful than ever. The crowd cheered wildly.

"That was Magic Wish Number One," said Arachne. "What next?"

Rachel looked hopefully at Grandy. "I wish someday I could find my Father, my Mother, and my big brother Tod," she said.

Again, Arachne covered her emerald-green eyes with her hands and chanted, "Spin, magic, spin!" This time she thrust her hands toward Rachel's three animal friends and tiny filaments of silken thread webbed around them.

Suddenly, Mister Elk was transformed into Rachel's Father! Mother Bird turned into Rachel's Mother! And Captain Toad became Rachel's brother Tod! Rachel and Grandy screamed with delight and the happy family members all began hugging one another.

While they were hugging, Rachel's Father explained what had happened. "Three years ago your Mother, brother Tod, and I had set out for the castle to ask the King to establish schools in the villages. But Arachne did not want the people of the Realm to be educated — that would have weakened her evil powers. So she turned us into forest creatures."

"As animals, we had no memory of our past lives," Rachel's Mother explained. "*CHIRP!* — oh, excuse me."

"So we didn't know what had happened until just now," added her brother Tod.

Rachel reflected for a moment. "That is why Arachne called you — I mean, my animal friends — her own creations," she reasoned.

"That is true," said Rachel's Father. "If she had not turned us into animals, we would never have been able to help you with the Three Impossible Tasks."

91

Rachel's Father, Mother and brother Tod appear magically.

"You cooked your own goose!" Grandy hollered at Arachne. Everyone laughed.

"Speaking of cooking, Sport," Tod said to Grandy, "did you bring any ginger cake with you to the castle?" He licked his lips and everyone chuckled.

"Ahem!" Arachne interrupted the happy family reunion. "That was Magic Wish Number Two. Rachel still has Magic Wish Number Three."

Rachel closed her eyes and pondered. Then she looked at Arachne and spoke quietly. "I wish that the precious treasures taken for the Three Impossible Tasks be returned to their rightful owners."

For a third time, Arachne covered her emerald-green eyes with her hands and chanted, "Spin, magic, spin!" Then she thrust her hands toward the three valuable treasures — the black pearl necklace, the Green Empress emerald, and the bronze bough with silver leaves and a golden apple — and tiny filaments of silken thread formed a web around each one.

Instantly, the magnificent black pearl necklace was carried to the Sea of Lusenta and fell magically around the neck of the Mermaid Princess. The breathtaking Green Empress emerald was lifted to the Kingdom of Rezonantz and dropped into the large hand of the Giant as he and his shivering cook climbed out of a snowdrift. And the precious bronze bough with silver leaves and a golden apple — which came from a tree in one of the King and Queen's Royal Forests, the Forest of Coriola — floated gently over to King Morland and Queen Allandra and settled softly into their arms.

The King and Queen gazed upon the treasure in amazement. Finally, King Morland spoke up. "This valuable treasure shall be used to purchase an even more valuable treasure for the Realm."

"Yes," said Queen Allandra. "It will be used to pay for schools throughout the land. No treasure is more valuable than an education." The crowd erupted in another cheer.

"What will happen to Arachne now that she's lost her evil powers?" Rachel asked King Morland. "I hope she won't be put to death."

"Do not worry, Rachel," assured the King. "Arachne shall not die. The Royal Magicians shall assign to her a task."

"A task?" asked Rachel.

"Yes," answered the King, "a very special task — it will be Arachne's last task. And she shall live in the most beautiful part of all the Realm."

"Thank you," said Rachel. *That is strange*, she thought to herself, *the most beautiful part of the Realm is the Royal Garden!*

As the Royal Guards took Arachne away to meet with the Royal Magicians, she flashed her emerald-green eyes at Rachel.

"Rachel," said King Morland, "the Queen and I would like you and your family to live with us here at the castle. We have extra rooms in the Royal Chambers. They are very nice."

Rachel glanced with excitement at her Father, Mother, Tod and Grandy. They were all smiling and nodding "yes." "Can our cat, Grindle, and my doll, Maggie, live here too?" she asked.

"Surely," replied the King.

"Thank you very much," said Rachel.

"Thank each of you for saving the Realm," answered the King.

"Now that we have settled that," said Queen Allandra, "we shall begin a festival of celebration in honor of Rachel — who proved that the most important thing in life is a kind heart."

CHAPTER EIGHT

The Last Task

RACHEL AND HER family moved into the castle chambers, where they lived in good health and happiness. The King and Queen kept their promise and established schools throughout the Realm. The birds of the Royal Forest watched over Mother Bird's babies, who soon learned to fly and take care of themselves. They often flew to the castle to visit Rachel's Mother and sing lovely melodies for visitors to the Royal Garden.

The Royal Garden was truly the most beautiful part of the Realm. Visitors from far and wide strolled along its winding paths through magnificent trees, lush plants and fragrant flowers. They marveled at the garden's splendor and were happy that it seemed to be so free from bothersome flies. In a far corner of the garden, visitors saw a small sign on a post. The sign read:

> *The Royal Garden*
> *Is Free From Flies*
> *By Courtesy Of*
> *The Royal Magicians.*

Arachne's last task.

Next to the sign, a silvery gossamer spider web — with dew drops that sparkled like diamonds — glistened magnificently in the sun. Looking closer at the web, visitors could see a velvety black widow spider with a ruby-red mark on her stomach. She was busily catching flies — for that was her task.

Visitors who looked very close noticed something unusual about the spider. For, unlike any other black widow spider they had ever seen, this black widow spider had beautifully strange eyes that almost seemed to glow. They were the color of emerald-green.

THE END